FAVOURITE FAIRY TALES

Licensed exclusively to Top That Publishing Ltd
Tide Mill Way, Woodbridge, Suffolk, IP12 1AP, UK
www.topthatpublishing.com
Copyright © 2015 Tide Mill Media
All rights reserved
2 4 6 8 9 7 5 3
Manufactured in China

Written by Kate Thomson
Illustrated by Alison Atkins

ISBN 978-1-78244-003-1

A catalogue record for this book is available from the British Library

One sunny day, a little girl named Goldilocks went for a walk. Soon, she came across a path that led to a pretty little cottage. Goldilocks wanted to find out who lived there, so she pushed the door open and went inside.

She found three bowls
of porridge on the table.
Goldilocks was hungry, so she
tasted some from the largest
bowl, but it was too hot.
The porridge in the middle-sized
bowl was too cold, but the
porridge in the smallest bowl
was delicious – so she ate it all up.

By then, Goldilocks was full up, and wanted to sit down. She found the living room, and saw three chairs. The wooden chair was hard, the armchair too soft, but the little chair was perfect. Just as she sat on it, it broke!

When Goldilocks went upstairs, she found three beds. The first was hard, the second was soft and very bouncy. After a while, Goldilocks felt very sleepy, and lay down on the third bed, which was warm and comfy.

Suddenly, Goldilocks awoke to find three grumpy-looking bears glaring at her! She was so scared that she screamed, and ran home. That day Goldilocks decided never to enter someone else's house without being invited first!

THE END

Once upon a time, there were Three Little Pigs. They lived comfortably at home with their mother. However, the day came when they had grown so big that there was no longer any room for them. It was time for them to leave.

The Three Little Pigs decided to build themselves a house each to live in. The First Little Pig built a house from straw. The Second Little Pig built a house from sticks. The Third Little Pig made his house from bricks. He took his time and was the last to finish!

Nearby lived a hungry wolf
who ate little pigs. He walked to
the house made of straw and puffed
his chest out. 'I'll huff and puff and
blow this house down,' he called to
the First Little Pig.
And he did! The First Little Pig was
so scared that he ran to hide in
the house made of sticks.

Then, the wolf walked to the house of sticks. The two little pigs were huddled together inside. 'I'll huff and puff and blow this house down,' cried the wolf. And he did! The two little pigs were so scared that they quickly let go of each other and ran as fast as they could to shelter in the house of bricks.

The Third Little Pig welcomed his brothers and let them in for a nice cup of tea. But the wolf wasn't far behind. 'I'll huff and puff and blow this house down,' cried the wolf. But the walls were so strong, that he couldn't! Thanks to the Third Little Pig's hard work, they were safe at last from the hungry wolf.